W9-BAA-653

Three Samurai Cats

A STORY FROM JAPAN

RETOLD BY

Eric A. Kimmel

ILLUSTRATED BY

Mordicai Gerstein

SCHOLASTIC INC.
New York Toronto London Auckland Sydney
Mexico City New Delhi Hong Kong Buenos Aires

There was once a daimyo, a powerful lord, whose castle was occupied by a savage rat. The daimyo tried everything in his power to chase the rat out. Nothing worked. The rat laughed at traps. He ignored poison. He even attacked the guard dogs.

"The castle is no longer my own!" the daimyo complained. "The rat is master here, not I. I must find a way to get rid of him."

The daimyo rode to a distant shrine famous for its corps of fighting samurai cats—tough, skilled fighters.

He entered and bowed to the dōchō, the senior monk.

"Dōchō, I need your help," he said. "A barbarous rat has taken over my castle. Send me a samurai cat to chase him out."

"I have just the one you need, but he is on another mission," the dōchō said. "He will be back in a few days. I will send him to you."

A few days later a samurai cat appeared at the castle gate.

"The dōchō sent me," the cat told the daimyo. "Where is the rat?"

"He is in the main hall. Follow me." The daimyo led the cat to the main hall of the castle. They found the rat twirling a fighting staff.

The samurai cat drew his sword. "Villain! I have come to drive you out."

"You're welcome to try," replied the rat.

The cat charged.

The rat leaped aside and thrust his staff between the cat's legs. The cat went sprawling.

"You'd better go," the rat said.

The humiliated cat bowed and left.

The daimyo rode back to the shrine. "Don't send me beginners," he told the dōchō. "It will take a real champion to defeat that rat."

"I have just the one," the dōchō replied. "Unfortunately, he is away on a journey. When he returns, I will send him to you."

Two weeks later another cat appeared. This one was twice as big as the first and armored from head to tail.

"Aha!" cried the daimyo. "A real samurai at last!"

He led the cat to the castle's main hall. The rat was practicing shadowboxing.

"You'll have to leave," the cat said.

"You'll have to throw me out," replied the rat.

"I can do that," said the cat.

"What makes you so sure?" the rat asked.

"Watch! I will demonstrate the technique of *karigane,* the wild goose, followed by *shimo-tatewari,* the bottom vertical split."

The samurai cat drew his sword and proceeded to put on an amazing display of swordsmanship.

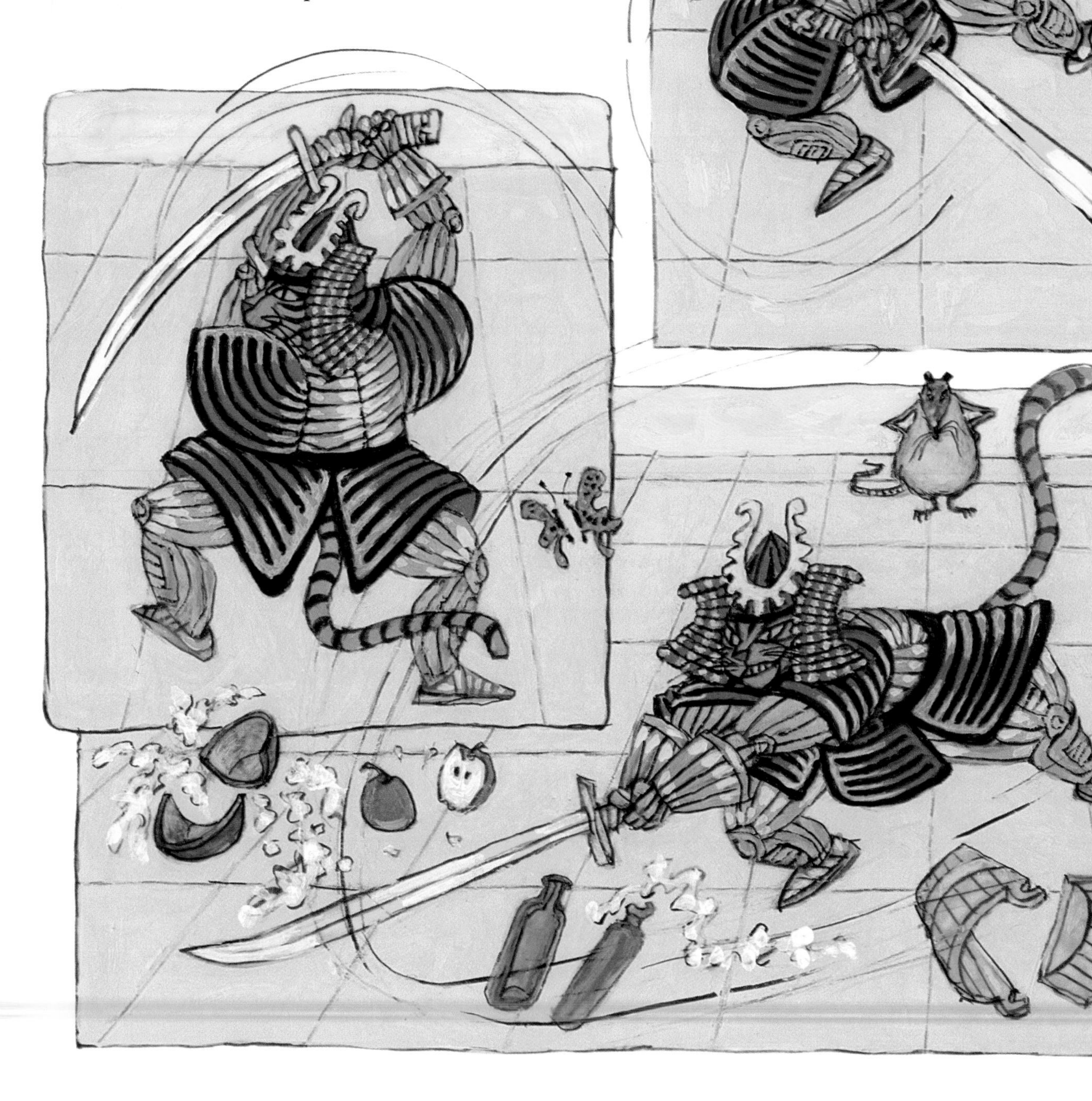

"Incredible!" the daimyo exclaimed.

"Can you do *ryo kuruma,* the big pair of wheels?" the rat asked.

"Of course." The cat sheathed his sword and prepared to begin.

Without warning, the rat leaped. He gave the cat a lightning kick that sent him flying across the hall.

"Not again!" the daimyo cried.

The cat regained his breath. He bowed to the rat and left.

"You may as well give up," the rat told the daimyo. "None of these cats can defeat me."

“We’re not done yet,” the daimyo snapped. He saddled his horse and rode back to the shrine.

"This is more serious than I thought," the dōchō said. "I will send for Neko Roshi."

"Who is that?" the daimyo asked.

"Neko Roshi is the greatest living master of the martial arts. He is on a retreat in the mountains. I will send him to you when he returns."

"I hope it's soon," the daimyo grumbled.

Five weeks later an elderly cat arrived at the castle gate. He wore a ragged kimono and worn-down *geta*, wooden clogs. He had no teeth. His tail was a mess. He walked with a limp.

"This is the most decrepit cat I ever saw!" the daimyo thought to himself. He was even more surprised when the cat said, "The dōchō sent me. I am Neko Roshi."

“You!” The daimyo laughed. “The dōchō must be joking.”

“The dōchō never jokes,” the cat said. “Is there a rat you wish to get rid of? I can do that, but it must be done my way.”

“As you wish,” the daimyo replied. “Would you like to see the rat? He is in the main hall, practicing stick fighting.”

"No," the cat sniffed. "However, I would like something to eat and a mat to sleep on."

The daimyo sent for a cushion and a bowl of fish and rice. The cat ate, licked his paws, lay down, and went to sleep.

The rat wandered in. “Do you want to fight?” he asked the cat.

The cat opened one eye, then closed it again. “Not today.”

“Tomorrow perhaps?”

“Perhaps,” the cat said.

The daimyo looked on in disgust. This cat was absolutely useless! The rat grew bolder than he had ever been. He taunted the servants. He took food from the kitchen. He sat in the daimyo's place and laughed at him.

"That's quite a tiger you have! Just looking at him terrifies me! Ha, ha, ha, ha, ha!"

Weeks passed. The cat did nothing but eat and sleep. The rat came by occasionally to ask if he wanted to fight. The answer was always no. Eventually, the rat stopped asking. He ran about the castle as he pleased. He took food from the cat's own dish. The cat never tried to stop him.

The daimyo could tolerate no more. He rode back to the shrine. “How dare you mock me?” he stormed at the dōchō. “Is that worthless cat supposed to be a samurai? He’s completely useless! A stuffed cat could do better!”

The dōchō answered: “Neko Roshi has his own way of doing things. Be patient. You will be rid of the rat soon.”

The daimyo returned in time for the Obon Festival. He found the cat still fast asleep, while the rat helped himself to the sticky rice balls being prepared for the holiday. He took all the rice balls from the daimyo's tray and stuck them together to make one huge rice ball. He rolled the rice ball across the floor to his rat hole. No one dared stop him. The daimyo watched in helpless fury.

The cat, as usual, did nothing.

Suddenly, the rat's foot caught on the edge of a tatami mat. He tripped and fell against the rice ball. The ball rolled over him, trapping the rat in sticky rice.

"Help!" the rat yelled.

The cat opened his eyes. His whiskers twitched. He arched his back, jumped off the cushion, and limped over to the rice ball.

"I'll help you," said the cat. "But you must promise to leave the castle."

"What if I don't?"

The cat purred. He extended one claw.

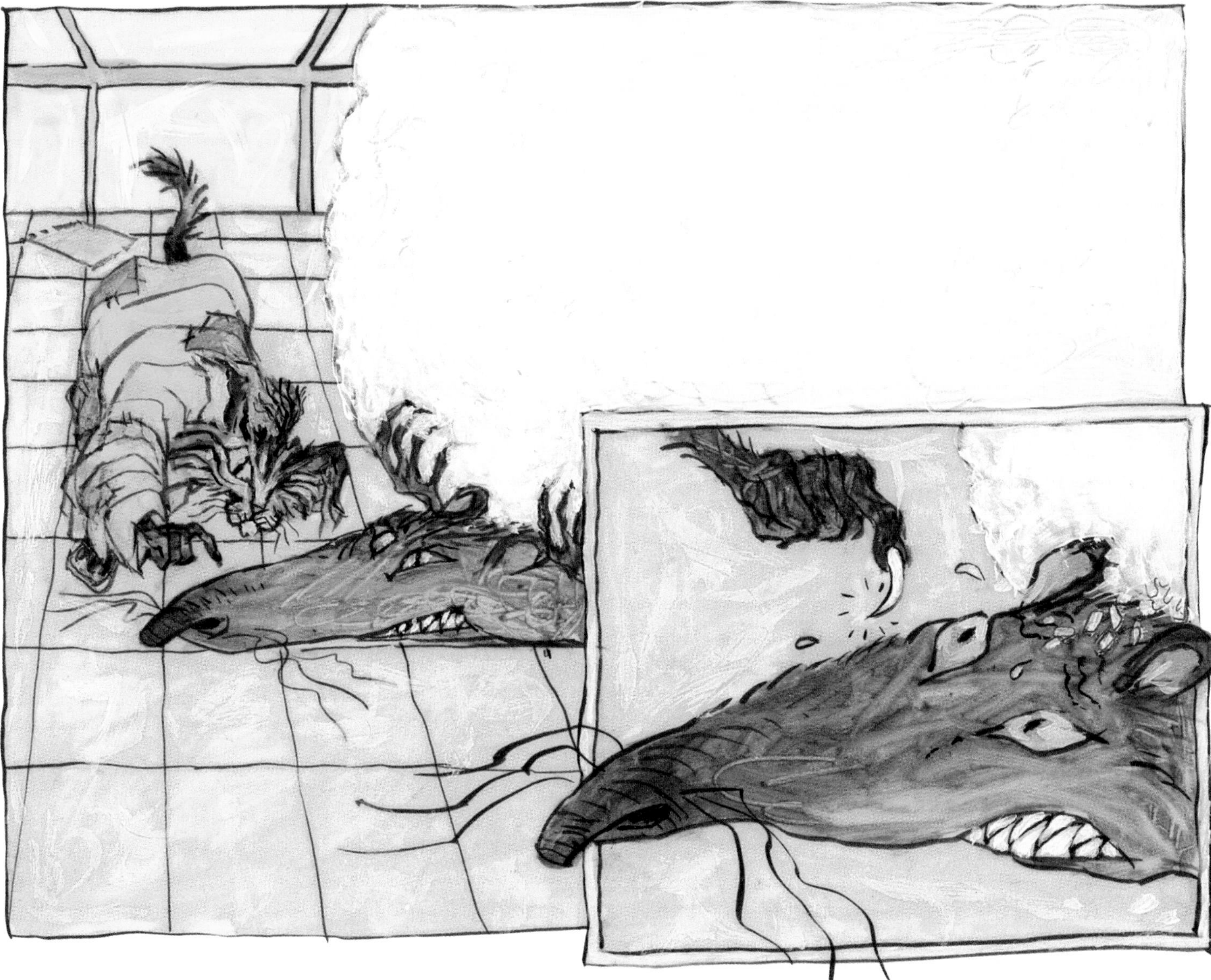

"I'll go," squeaked the rat. And he did.

The daimyo brought a rich present to the shrine. "What I still don't understand," he remarked to the dōchō, "is how that decrepit old cat could succeed where two young samurai failed completely?"

"There is no mystery," the dōchō replied. "The first two cats tried to overcome the rat with force. Neko Roshi, on the other hand, allowed his opponent to defeat himself. It is the lesson we teach here all the time, though few ever truly understand it."

"And that lesson is?" asked the daimyo.

"Draw strength from stillness. Learn to act without acting. And never underestimate a samurai cat. Especially when he is old and you are a rat who likes rice balls."

AUTHOR'S NOTE

If this story seems strange, perhaps that is the point. The Zen masters used similar stories and sayings to surprise their disciples out of conventional patterns of thinking.

The samurai were the knights of medieval Japan. Most followed the practices and teachings of Zen Buddhism, which emphasized stillness, meditation, and harmony with nature. Many Buddhist shrines maintained formidable armies of fighting monks who developed the techniques that became the Japanese martial arts.

A *daimyo* is a feudal lord. A *dōchō* is the senior monk, the abbot of a monastery. *Neko* is a cat. A *roshi* is a Zen master, one who has achieved enlightenment. *Geta* are wooden clogs.

I adapted this story from a version found in Gerald and Loretta Hausman's *The Mythology of Cats: Feline Legend and Lore Through the Ages* (New York: St. Martin's Press, 1998). The Hausmans cite Kenji Sora's *The Swordsman and the Cat* as their source.

To Mordicai, that cool cat — E. A. K.

For Hugh, who could be a great samurai, or anything else
he might choose — Grandpa (M. G.)

No part of this publication may be reproduced in whole or in part,
or stored in a retrieval system, or transmitted in any form or by any means,
electronic, mechanical, photocopying, recording, or otherwise, without written
permission of the publisher. For information regarding permission, write to
Holiday House, Inc., 425 Madison Avenue,
New York, NY 10017.

ISBN 0-439-69256-3

Text copyright © 2003 by Eric A. Kimmel. Illustrations copyright
© 2003 by Mordicai Gerstein. All rights reserved. Published by Scholastic Inc.,
557 Broadway, New York, NY 10012, by arrangement with Holiday House, Inc.
SCHOLASTIC and associated logos are
trademarks and/or registered trademarks of Scholastic Inc.

12 11 10 9 8 7 6 5 4 3 2 1 4 5 6 7 8 9/0

Printed in the U.S.A. 40

First Scholastic printing, March 2004

The text typeface is Hiroshige.
The illustrations were created using pen and ink with oil paint
on heavy vellum paper.